Nature Trail

Benjamin Zephaniah • Nila Aye

ORCHARD

At the bottom of my garden . . .

For all the animals in my garden.
For the animals in the seas, in the skies, and on the Earth.
I hope we can live together for ever.
I hope we can live. – **B.Z.**

For my son Tom, my very own nature boy, who made me
see the world through new eyes again. Thank you x – **N.A.**

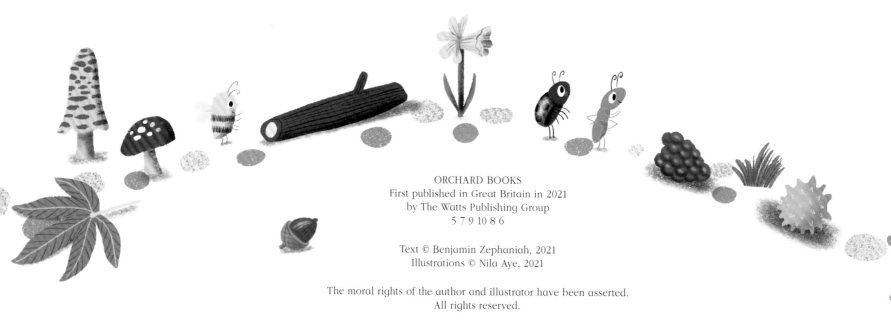

ORCHARD BOOKS
First published in Great Britain in 2021
by The Watts Publishing Group
5 7 9 10 8 6

Text © Benjamin Zephaniah, 2021
Illustrations © Nila Aye, 2021

A CIP catalogue record for this book is available from the British Library.

HB ISBN 978 1 40836 125 2
PB ISBN 978 1 40836 126 9

Printed in Italy

Orchard Books
An imprint of Hachette Children's Group
Part of The Watts Publishing Group Limited
Carmelite House, 50 Victoria Embankment,
London EC4Y 0DZ

An Hachette UK Company
www.hachette.co.uk
www.hachettechildrens.co.uk

There's a hedgehog and a frog,

And a lot of creepy-crawlies
Living underneath a log.

There's a baby daddy-longlegs
And an easy-going snail,
And a family of woodlice –
All are on my nature trail.

There are caterpillars waiting
For their time to come to fly,
There are worms turning the earth over
As ladybirds fly by.

Birds will visit,
cats will visit,
But they always
choose their time . . .

And I've even seen a fox visit
This wild garden of mine.

Squirrels come to nick my nuts
And busy bees come buzzing . . .

And when the night time comes,
Sometimes some dragonflies come humming.

My garden mice are very shy,
And I've seen bats that growl.
And in my garden, I have seen
A very wise old owl.

My garden is a lively place,
There's always something happening.

There's this constant search for food
And then there's all that flowering.

When you have a garden

You will never be alone . . .

And I believe we all deserve
A garden of our own.